CAPTAIN PUGWASH

A Pirate Story

by

JOHN RYAN

F

FRANCES LINCOLN
CHILDREN'S BOOKS

Captain Pugwash was a pirate. He thought himself the bravest, most handsome pirate on the seven seas.   Here is a portrait of him.

He had a ship called *The Black Pig*, with a crew that was the laziest afloat, and a Mate who was always fast asleep.

He had, too, a cabin boy called Tom, and
this was lucky, because Tom was really the
only person aboard who knew how to work
the compass, sail the ship, and make the tea.

One sunny morning, Captain Pugwash
was happily steering his ship through the blue
Caribbean Sea, looking, as usual, for treasure.
The mate was asleep, of course, and the crew
were all busy . . .

lying about the deck,
playing games,
and watching the clouds
and the waves
and the
fishes.

The Captain had a map

to show him where the treasure was
and to help him to steer clear of sea monsters and storms.

The only thing that really worried Captain Pugwash was the danger of meeting other pirates. One of these, whose name was Cut-throat Jake, was so fierce that the very thought of him was enough to make Captain Pugwash want to give up sailing and take to market gardening instead.

Cut-throat Jake was a very bad man indeed. Everyone said that his heart was blacker than his beard. He had an enormous ship, bristling with guns, and worst of all, he simply hated Captain Pugwash.

The Captain was just
thinking about this when
there was a loud cry from
the crow's nest, where Tom,
who was keeping a look-
out with his telescope,
had just spotted a ship.
'SHIP AHOY!'
shouted Tom—so loudly
that it made the Captain
jump, and almost woke up
the mate.

'What sort of ship?' cried Captain Pugwash, rushing anxiously to the side. 'Does it look like a treasure ship?'

'It looks a funny sort of ship to me,' said Tom as he climbed down the rigging.

'I can't see anybody on board, and there's a lot of yellow stuff lying in a shining heap on the deck.'

'What!' shouted the Captain, seizing the telescope. 'Good gracious me—it's TREASURE—and no one to guard it! Lower the dinghy—I'm going aboard!'

'All by yourself, Cap'n?' said Tom. 'And why not, boy?' said Pugwash. 'There's nobody to fight, and besides, if I go alone, all the treasure will belong to me.'

'Please, Cap'n,' said Tom, 'Wouldn't it be safer if I went too? I shan't want any of the treasure, and—well you know *you* aren't very good at rowing . . .'

'Oh, very well,' grunted the Captain.

It was never easy getting him out of a big boat into a small one, but in the end they managed it, and away they went.

Over on the other ship, Cut-throat Jake laughed softly into his enormous beard, and waited . . .

For years he had been trying to catch Pugwash. He had never succeeded because the Captain was so frightened of him that he always ran away long before Jake could get anywhere near him. Then Jake had suddenly thought of a wonderful plan. He had disguised his ship and waited for *The Black Pig* to come near. Then he had scattered gold and precious stones all over the deck, and hidden himself and his crew.

✳   ✳   ✳   ✳

'Faster, boy! Faster!' cried the Captain as Tom rowed closer and closer to the strange ship.

At last they reached it. A rope ladder was hanging conveniently over the side, and Pugwash heaved himself on to the deck. And when he got there, he could hardly believe his eyes.

There was gold and silver and precious stones galore and, waiting down below, Tom could hear the Captain's exclamations of delight as he gazed at the sparkling treasure.

Then, suddenly, Tom heard a different sort of noise . . .

'Yo ho, ho ho!' shouted Cut-throat Jake
as he rushed out from behind a huge coil of rope.

'Ya ha, ha ha!' yelled Jake's pirates,
leaping out of all the hatchways in sight.

And—'HELP!' cried Pugwash in a very
weak voice, as they grabbed him.

'Got you at last!' said Jake. 'Even if it has taken me twenty years. Now, men— what shall we do with him?'

'The plank! The plank! Make him walk the plank!' shouted all the pirates together.

'And a very good idea too,' said Jake. 'And since you're so fond of treasure, Cap'n, we'll fill your pockets with the stuff. It will make you sink more quickly.'

So they stuffed poor Pugwash's pockets with gold and silver and precious stones, and filled his boots too, to make him heavier still. Then they pushed him on to the plank, and the Captain wished very much that he had never gone to sea.

But there was one thing he and Jake and all the pirates on Jake's ship had forgotten—and that was Tom, waiting down below in the little rowing boat.

'Off you go, Cap'n,' said Jake, 'It was so nice of you to drop in.' And Pugwash started to totter very unsteadily along the plank. If there was one thing he hated it was cold water.

'Go on,' shouted Jake, 'Hurry up! We can't wait all day, you know.'

Pugwash hesitated, held his nose, lost his balance, and toppled off the end of the plank . . .

'That's the last time you'll drop in anywhere!' shouted Cut-throat Jake—and all the pirates thought this such a good joke that they sat down and roared with laughter for about five minutes. In fact, they were all so busy laughing that none of them saw what really happened. When Pugwash landed in the water, Tom was ready for him, and he pulled the Captain head-first into the dinghy and rowed away as fast as he could.

So when Jake went to the side of the
ship to have another look, this is what he saw.

And when he saw it, he was so angry that he almost burst with rage, and used such terribly bad language that even the wickedest of his crew blushed. 'Get out the cannon!' roared Jake; but as all the cannon and cannon-balls and gunpowder had been hidden, it was a long time before the pirates were ready to fire.

The first shot missed and the second and third shots missed, and then Cut-throat Jake got so angry that he chose an extra large cannon-ball, to make quite sure of hitting the little boat this time.

But . . .

it was too big.

It stuck in the cannon, and when they let it off, the whole thing exploded with a fearful bang which knocked Cut-throat Jake and all his crew senseless.

Meanwhile, aboard *The Black Pig*, Captain Pugwash's pirates were roused by the sudden noise, and rushed to see what was happening.

'It's the Cap'n!' shouted the Mate, rubbing the sleep from his eyes. 'Stand by with the boat-hook!'

So Captain Pugwash came back to his ship again
and stood in triumph on his own quarter-
deck, and *The Black Pig* sailed away as fast
as possible from Cut-throat Jake's ship.

'Smart work, eh,' said the Captain to his admiring crew, as they watched him emptying all the treasure which Jake had given him.

'That old ruffian thought he'd caught me, but I was too clever for him! Ha! It takes more than a silly scallywag like Cut-throat Jake to catch me.'

'Oh well,' thought Tom to himself, as he curled up to sleep in his hammock that night—'It's lucky there was *somebody* there to catch him!'

The End

Copyright © John Ryan 1957
First published in 1957 by The Bodley Head Ltd
This edition published in Great Britain in 2008 by
Frances Lincoln Children's Books, 4 Torriano Mews,
Torriano Avenue, London NW5 2RZ
www.franceslincoln.com

ISBN: 978-1-84507-919-2

Printed in Heshan, Guangdong, China by Leo Paper Products Ltd.
in December 2009

3 5 7 9 8 6 4 2